Milly and Molly

For my grandchildren
Thomas, Harry, Ella and Madeleine

Published by
Milly Molly Books
P O Box 539
Gisborne, New Zealand
email: books@millymolly.com

Printed by Rhythm Consolidated Berhad, Malaysia

ISBN: 1-86972-015-6

10   9   8   7   6   5   4   3   2   1

Milly, Molly
and
Sock Heaven

"We may look different
but we feel the same."

Milly's dad was desperate. "I'll hug anyone who can find my missing sock. Anyone!" he said.

He had been through the clothes basket,

looked in the washing machine

and down behind the dryer.

He had looked under his bed

and in the toe of his boots.

He had turned his sock drawer over twice

and searched high and low.

Milly and Molly had never seen him so
miserable. And they'd never heard him say
he would hug just anyone. That was the
bit that worried them the most.
Who had gone off with his sock?

They checked out the postman.

They asked Aunt Maude politely to lift her skirt.

They pleaded with Old Frosty to stretch
up and pick them an apple.

The butcher's socks came up to his knees

and Mr. Limpy said, "I have a similar problem."

Miss Blythe said, "socks make my feet itchy."

And Farmer Hegarty's socks looked far
too big and woolly.

Doctor Smiley's socks were black.

BushBob's socks were stripped.

Father Brownlie said, "I don't wear socks and, besides, everyone knows socks don't go missing. They just collect in sock heaven."

Molly's mother said, "I haven't seen a blue sock in the wash."

And Milly's mother said, "I've never known anyone to lose more socks. I'll bet it's still in his sock drawer!"

Late that night Milly's dad turned out
the lights and put Marmalade to bed.

And there it was! His blue sock. He told
Marmalade she was the best cat and gave
her a great, big hug.

Milly, Molly and SockHeaven

The value implicitly expressed in this story is 'helpfulness' - making something easy, better or quicker for someone.

Milly and Molly were very helpful in asking everyone if they had seen the missing sock. They wanted to help Milly's dad find his sock.

"We may look different but we feel the same."

Milly Molly®

B O O K S

Other picture books in the Milly, Molly series include:

- Milly, Molly and Jimmy's Seeds   ISBN 1-86972-000-8

- Milly, Molly and Beefy   ISBN 1-86972-006-7

- Milly, Molly and Pet Day   ISBN 1-86972-004-0

- Milly, Molly and Oink   ISBN 1-86972-002-4

- Milly and Molly Go Camping   ISBN 1-86972-003-2

- Milly, Molly and Betelgeuse   ISBN 1-86972-005-9

- Milly, Molly and Taffy Bogle   ISBN 1-86972-001-6

- Milly, Molly and Aunt Maude   ISBN 1-86972-014-8

- Milly, Molly and Alf   ISBN 1-86972-018-0

- Milly, Molly and the Sunhat   ISBN 1-86972-016-4

- Milly, Molly and Special Friends   ISBN 1-86972-017-2

- Milly, Molly and Different Dads   ISBN 1-86972-019-9